YOU AND YOUR CHILD

PLAYDOUGH

Ray Gibson and Jenny Tyler

Illustrated by Simone Abel
and Graham Round

Designed by Carol Law

Edited by Robyn Gee

Photography by Lesley Howling

About this book

Playing with playdough gives children opportunities to develop useful skills such as hand control, coordination, planning and decision-making. Most young children need little encouragement to start poking, rolling and squeezing the dough. But, as time goes by, the more you can supply in the way of tools and ideas, the more they will learn from it. This book is designed to give you some starting points.

First published in 1989 by Usborne Publishing Ltd,
Usborne House, 83-85 Saffron Hill,
London EC1N 8RT, England.
Copyright © 1989 Usborne Publishing Ltd.
The name Usborne and the device 🎈 are Trade Marks of Usborne Publishing Ltd. All rights

Caterpillar on a leaf

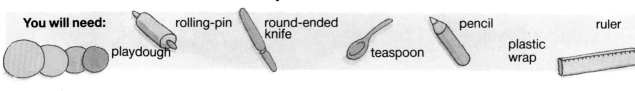

You will need: rolling-pin, round-ended knife, playdough, teaspoon, pencil, plastic wrap, ruler

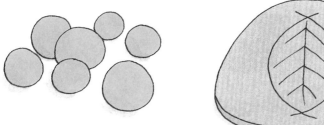

Roll seven or eight balls of different sizes.

Roll out some green dough on plastic wrap. Using a knife, cut out a leaf shape and mark veins on it.

Position the balls in a row on the leaf, starting with the biggest and ending with the smallest.

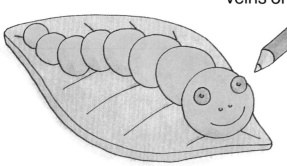

Roll two small balls of dough for eyes. Press them onto the head with the pointed end of a pencil. Make two pencil holes for nostrils and mark in the mouth with the end of a teaspoon.

Other ideas

Ladybird
Flatten a ball of dough, then press the side of a ruler across the centre.

Press on small flattened balls for spots and eyes.

Roll two small antennae.

Attach head.

Poke small white balls into centre of each eye with a pencil point.

Mark mouth with side of spoon.

Mark in nostrils with a pencil point.

Bee
Flatten three balls of dough and press them together. Fix on a round head and a pointed tail.

Press on eyes with a pencil point.

Add two pear-shaped wings.

Mark nostrils and mouth.

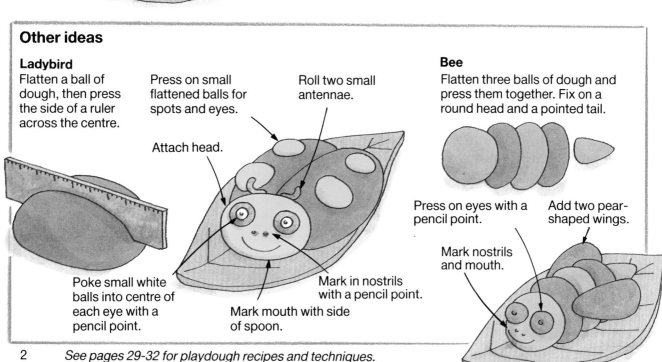

See pages 29-32 for playdough recipes and techniques.

Snowman by a pond

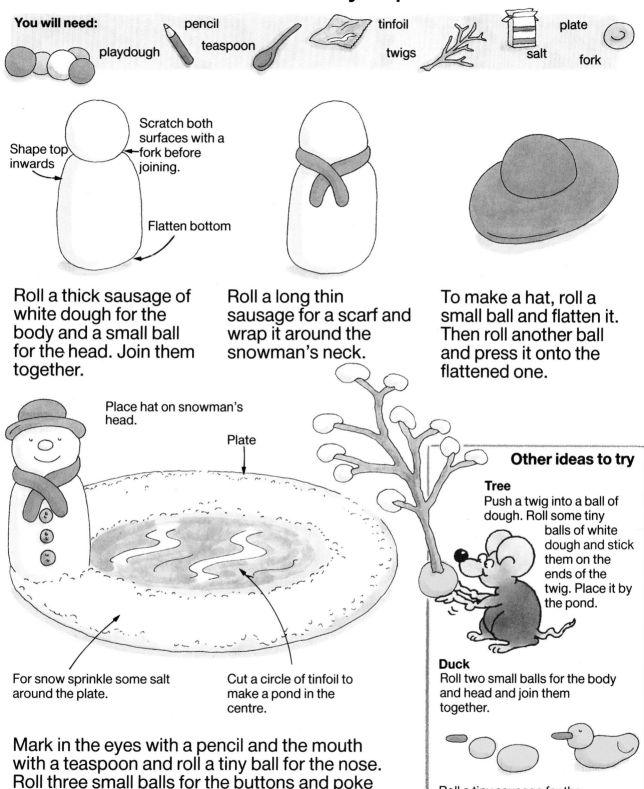

You will need: playdough, pencil, teaspoon, tinfoil, twigs, plate, salt, fork

Shape top inwards

Scratch both surfaces with a fork before joining.

Flatten bottom

Roll a thick sausage of white dough for the body and a small ball for the head. Join them together.

Roll a long thin sausage for a scarf and wrap it around the snowman's neck.

To make a hat, roll a small ball and flatten it. Then roll another ball and press it onto the flattened one.

Place hat on snowman's head.

Plate

For snow sprinkle some salt around the plate.

Cut a circle of tinfoil to make a pond in the centre.

Mark in the eyes with a pencil and the mouth with a teaspoon and roll a tiny ball for the nose. Roll three small balls for the buttons and poke each one twice with a pencil. Place the snowman on the plate.

Other ideas to try

Tree
Push a twig into a ball of dough. Roll some tiny balls of white dough and stick them on the ends of the twig. Place it by the pond.

Duck
Roll two small balls for the body and head and join them together.

Roll a tiny sausage for the beak. Pinch out a tail. Put the duck on the pond.

3

Pigs in a pen

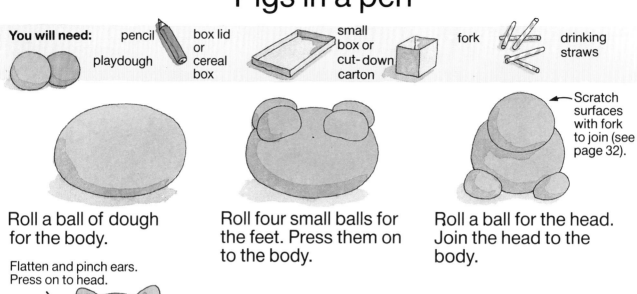

Roll a ball of dough for the body.

Roll four small balls for the feet. Press them on to the body.

Roll a ball for the head. Join the head to the body.

Scratch surfaces with fork to join (see page 32).

Flatten and pinch ears. Press on to head.

Press on snout.

Roll two small balls for the ears and one for the snout.

Roll a thin sausage for the tail.

Mark holes for the eyes and snout with a pencil.

Pig pen and cabbages

You could make several pigs and then make a pen for them.

Cut a doorway in the small box, or cut-down carton. Put it upside down inside the box lid to make a shed.

Cut up some paper or drinking straws for the pigs to lie on.

Make some tiny baby pigs too.

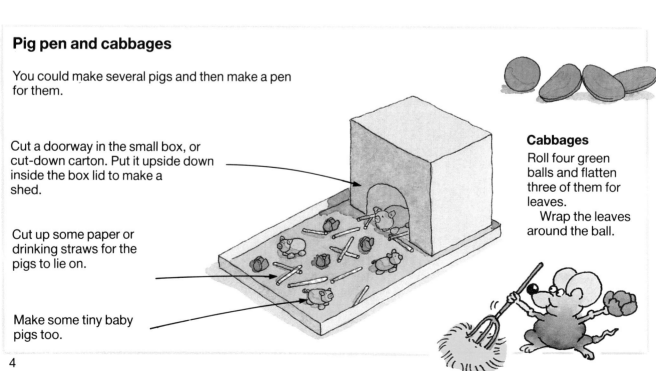

Cabbages
Roll four green balls and flatten three of them for leaves.
Wrap the leaves around the ball.

Sheep in a field

You will need:

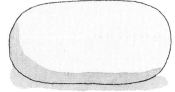 playdough   pencil   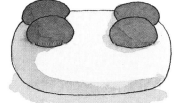 fork and round-ended knife   box lid or cereal box    sieve or garlic press   paint

Roll a fat sausage of dough for the body.

Roll four small balls for the feet and press them on.

Roll a fat sausage for the head and fix it to the body.

Roll two smaller sausages for the ears.

Make a short, fat, sausage for the tail.

Mark holes for nose and eyes with a pencil.

Mark body with a fork to give it a woolly look.

Field, flowers and bushes

You can use a box lid or cut-down cereal box to make a field for your sheep.

Make flowers in the same way as cabbages, using pink dough. Press the petals outwards.

Paint or crayon your box green, if you like, and draw a fence round it.

Make a lying down sheep by leaving the feet off.

Wet sieve first.

Push with thumbs through side of sieve. Scrape off with a knife.

Bushes
Try pushing green dough through a sieve to make bushes. This will only work if your dough is quite soft. If it is too stiff try squeezing it through a garlic press.

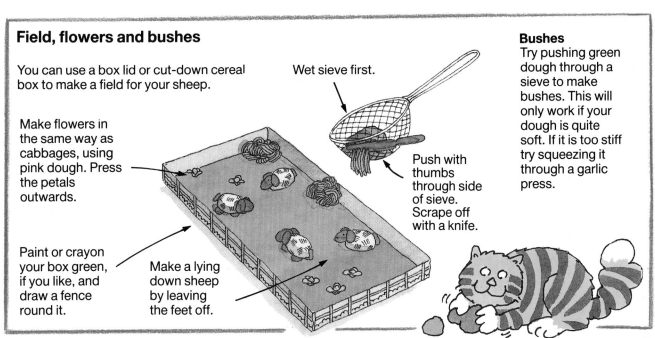

Cat on a cushion

You will need: pencil, rolling-pin, felt-tip pen, straw, saltdough*, lightly oiled baking tray, paint, round-ended knife, plastic wrap

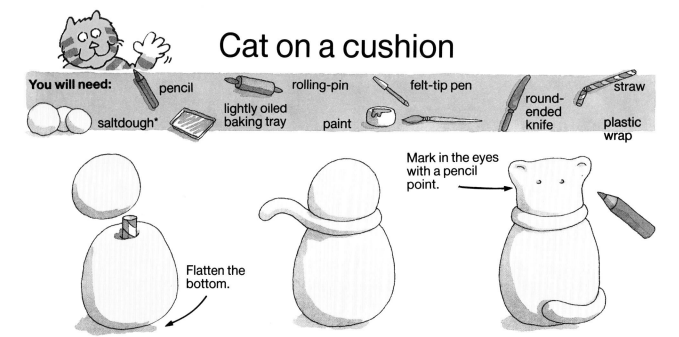

Flatten the bottom.

Mark in the eyes with a pencil point.

Roll a ball of dough for the body. Press in a piece of straw. Attach a smaller ball for the head.

Roll a thin sausage of dough for the collar and wrap it around the neck.

Roll a thicker sausage for the tail. Press it on and wrap it round. Pinch out the ears.

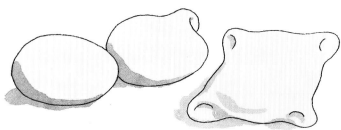

Mark in the face with felt-tip pen.

Roll a ball of dough and flatten it in the palm of your hand.
Pinch out the sides to make four corners. Sit the cat on the cushion.

Bake in the oven before painting.*

Cat on a mat and other ideas

Roll out some dough on plastic wrap and cut an oblong shape.

Lay the body of the cat on the mat before adding the head and tail.

Press patterns in it with a straw and decorate the edges with a knife.

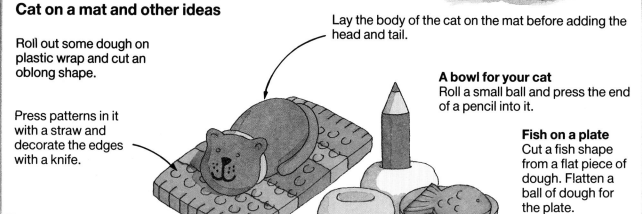

A bowl for your cat
Roll a small ball and press the end of a pencil into it.

Fish on a plate
Cut a fish shape from a flat piece of dough. Flatten a ball of dough for the plate.

*To find out how to make, bake and decorate saltdough, see page 30.

Sausage dog

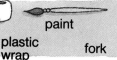

Scratch surfaces with fork to join (see page 5)

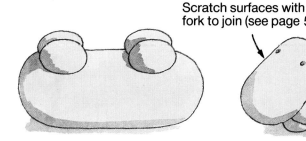

Roll a long, fat sausage of dough for the body and press on four small balls for feet.

Roll a short, fat sausage for the head. Join it to the body. Mark in the eyes with a pencil.

Roll two small sausages and flatten them to make ears. Join them to the top of the head.

Roll a small sausage for the tail and a tiny ball of dough for the nose. Press them on.

Mark in the whiskers with a pencil point and the mouth with a teaspoon. Bake your dog and then paint it.

Other ideas

A bowl
Make a bowl for your dog exactly as you make the cat's bowl, opposite. Write the dog's name on it.

A bone
Roll a small sausage and squeeze it in the middle. Make a slit at each end with a knife.

A kennel
Cut down a clean milk carton. Cut out a doorway, making sure your dog can fit through it.

Dog biscuits
Flatten lots of small balls of dough, then prick them with a pencil point.

*To find out how to make, bake and decorate saltdough, see page 30.

Baby in a matchbox

You will need: pencil, rolling-pin, paint, paper towels, cotton batting, plastic wrap, saltdough*, empty matchbox, felt-tip pen, glue, wool, scissors

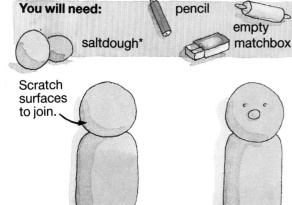

Scratch surfaces to join.

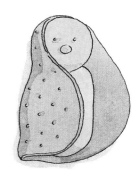

Roll a small ball for the head and a sausage for the body. Join them together.

Mark in the eyes with a pencil. Roll a tiny ball for the nose.

For the blanket, roll out a piece of dough on plastic wrap. Make markings with a pencil point.

Peel off the plastic wrap, turn the blanket over and wrap it round the baby.

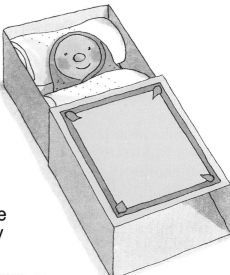

Bake and then paint the baby. Mark on its mouth with a felt-tip pen.

Cut three small pieces of paper towel to make a sheet, pillow and blanket.
  Place the sheet and pillow in the matchbox. Put the baby in and lay the blanket over the baby.

Other things to try

Baby's bottle
Roll a thin sausage for the bottle. Squash a small ball and place it on top. Roll a tiny sausage for the nipple. Bake and paint.

Mouse in a matchbox
Roll a small ball of dough. Pinch out a nose. Stick a tiny ball on the end.

Flatten two balls for ears and press them on with the end of a pencil. Bake and

cotton batting

paint, then glue on a wool tail.

Snail family

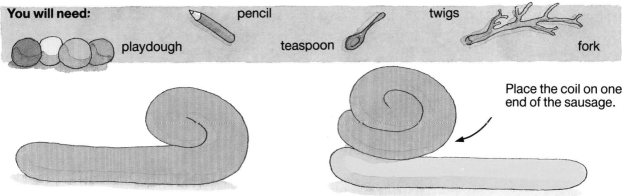

Place the coil on one end of the sausage.

Roll a long, fat sausage of dough into a coil to make the snail's shell.

Roll a shorter sausage and place the coil on top of it.

Bend up the ends and press to the coil. Bend the longer end forward to make a head.

Press on two balls for eyes with a pencil. Mark in the mouth with a teaspoon.

Decorate your snail by pressing little pieces of dough of another colour all over him.
Make a family of snails of various sizes.

Ideas for snakes

To make snakes roll long sausages of dough. Mark in their eyes with a pencil and mouths with a teaspoon.

Snakes in a basket

For the base of the basket, flatten a ball of dough.

Roll a long thin sausage. Press one end to the edge of the base and coil around.

You may have to make another sausage. Simply press it on where the first one ended and continue coiling.

Arrange some snakes in your basket.

Snake in a tree
Wind your snake around a twig.

These look good on window-ledges.

Hedgehog

Roll a ball of dough and pinch out a snout.

Add four balls of dough for feet.

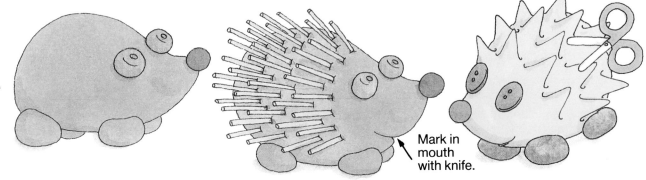

Add lentils, beads or buttons for eyes and a tiny ball of dough for the nose.

Starting from the front, press in spaghetti "quills". Or you can snip the dough with scissors for a spiky effect.

Mark in mouth with knife.

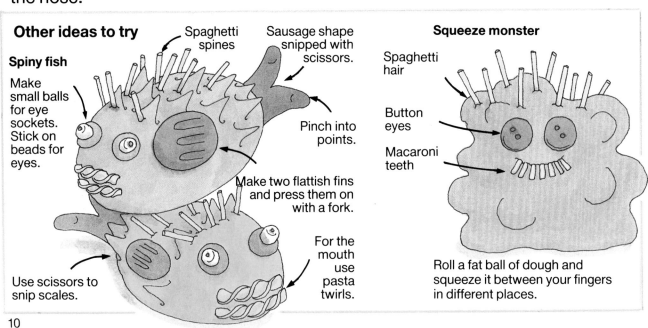

Other ideas to try

Spiny fish

Spaghetti spines

Sausage shape snipped with scissors.

Make small balls for eye sockets. Stick on beads for eyes.

Pinch into points.

Make two flattish fins and press them on with a fork.

Use scissors to snip scales.

For the mouth use pasta twirls.

Squeeze monster

Spaghetti hair

Button eyes

Macaroni teeth

Roll a fat ball of dough and squeeze it between your fingers in different places.

Dragon

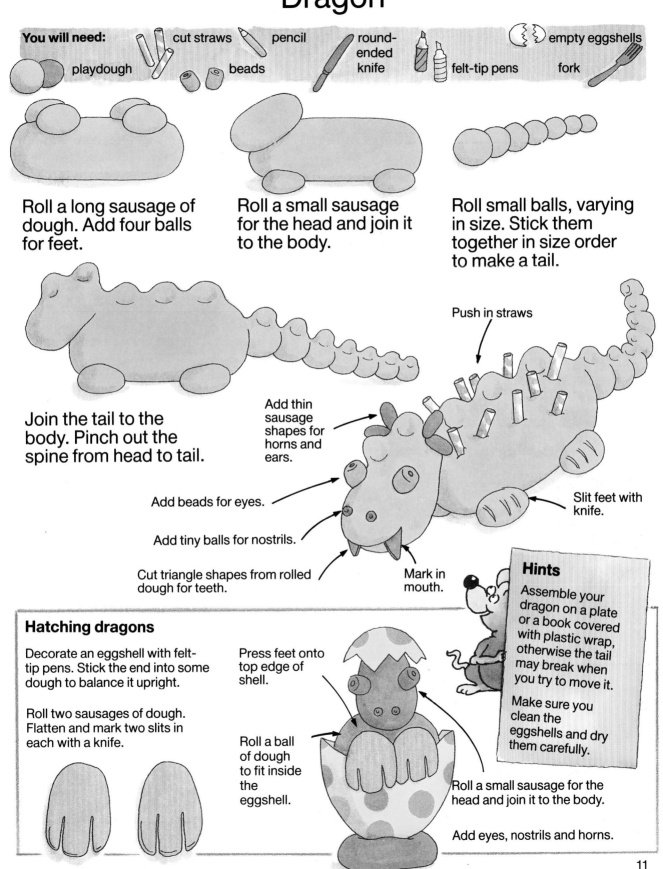

Roll a long sausage of dough. Add four balls for feet.

Roll a small sausage for the head and join it to the body.

Roll small balls, varying in size. Stick them together in size order to make a tail.

Join the tail to the body. Pinch out the spine from head to tail.

Add thin sausage shapes for horns and ears.

Push in straws

Add beads for eyes.

Slit feet with knife.

Add tiny balls for nostrils.

Cut triangle shapes from rolled dough for teeth.

Mark in mouth.

Hints

Assemble your dragon on a plate or a book covered with plastic wrap, otherwise the tail may break when you try to move it.

Make sure you clean the eggshells and dry them carefully.

Hatching dragons

Decorate an eggshell with felt-tip pens. Stick the end into some dough to balance it upright.

Roll two sausages of dough. Flatten and mark two slits in each with a knife.

Press feet onto top edge of shell.

Roll a ball of dough to fit inside the eggshell.

Roll a small sausage for the head and join it to the body.

Add eyes, nostrils and horns.

11

Jewelry

You will need: 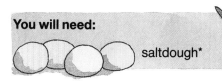 saltdough*  knitting needle / cookie cutters  paint  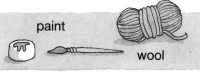 wool  pasta shapes

Bead necklace

Roll a sausage and cut it into pieces.

Poke the knitting needle through their centres.

Put the beads upright on a baking tray and bake them.

Paint the beads in bright colours.

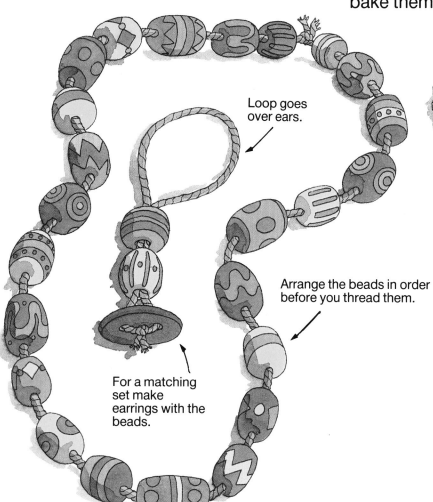

Loop goes over ears.

Arrange the beads in order before you thread them.

For a matching set make earrings with the beads.

Thread the beads, using wool, shoelaces or ribbon.

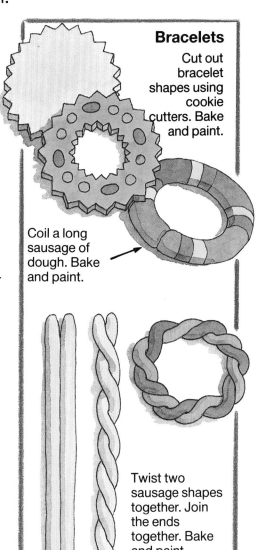

Bracelets

Cut out bracelet shapes using cookie cutters. Bake and paint.

Coil a long sausage of dough. Bake and paint.

Twist two sausage shapes together. Join the ends together. Bake and paint.

*To find out how to make, bake and decorate saltdough, see page 30.

 lightly-oiled baking tray pencil round-ended knife 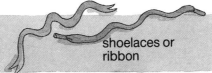 shoelaces or ribbon adhesive bandage safety pin

Teddy earrings

Roll a small ball of dough and flatten for the teddy's head.

Flatten three smaller balls for ears and nose. Join them to the head.

Mark the eyes with a pencil and make a hole at the top.

Tie a ribbon through the hole.

Bake and paint the earring. Mark in a nose and mouth with felt-tip pens.

Hints

Take care to make the holes big enough as the dough will shrink when baked.

For small things like this bake for only 10 to 15 minutes.

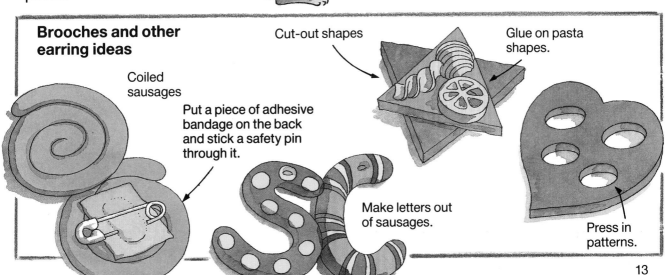

Brooches and other earring ideas

Coiled sausages

Cut-out shapes

Glue on pasta shapes.

Put a piece of adhesive bandage on the back and stick a safety pin through it.

Make letters out of sausages.

Press in patterns.

13

Playdough people

Man

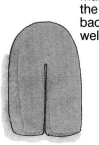

Mark the back as well.

Add a tiny ball for the nose.

Tiny balls poked in with pencil.

Thin sausage for belt.

Press buckle on with a blunt pencil.

Roll a long, thick sausage. Mark his legs by pressing a knife lightly along half his length.

Roll two sausage-shaped arms and small balls for hands. Add two balls for his feet.

Roll a ball for his head. Mark in his eyes with a pencil and his mouth with a teaspoon.

For his hair, cut tiny strips of dough, or press some dough through a garlic press.

Woman

See hint on joining pieces together.

Buttons pressed on with pencil.

Thin sausage for belt.

Decorate skirt with a pen top.

Hints

Secure head to body by pushing in a piece of straw.

Try putting the arms in different positions, or carefully bending the legs, so that your people can sit down.

Roll a thick sausage for her lower body. Add a smaller shape for her chest.

Add her head, arms and feet, as above, and mark in her face.

Give her some hair, then cut a triangle from rolled dough as a scarf.

Other ideas to try

Bags and baskets
For a basket, poke in the centre of a ball of dough with the end of a pencil. For the bag flatten a ball of dough. Make the handles from thin sausages.

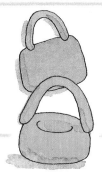

Hats
Flatten balls of dough with a finger. Roll small balls and place on top, then squash into shape.

Child in bed

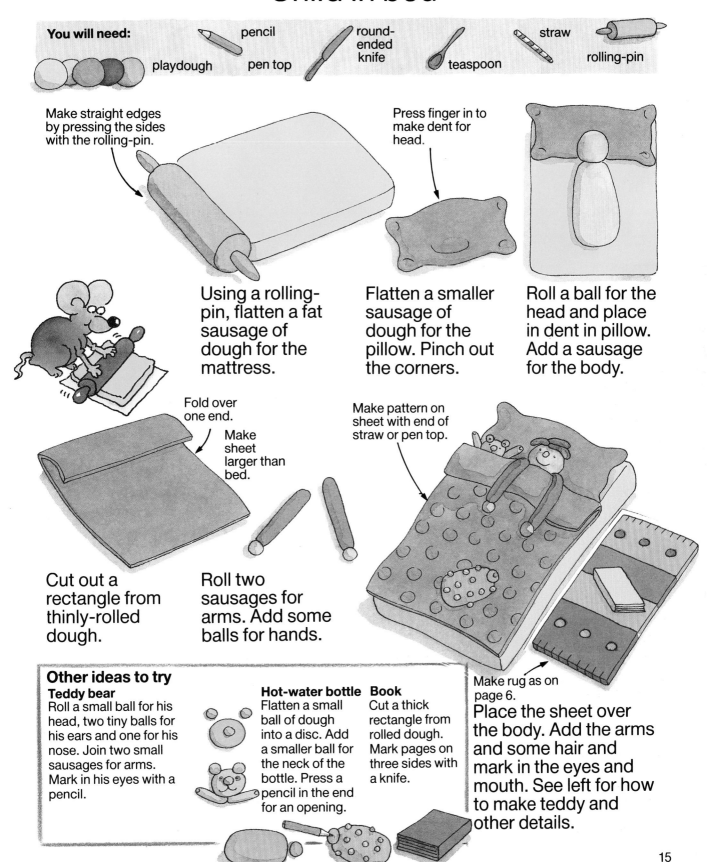

You will need: pencil, playdough, pen top, round-ended knife, teaspoon, straw, rolling-pin

Make straight edges by pressing the sides with the rolling-pin.

Press finger in to make dent for head.

Using a rolling-pin, flatten a fat sausage of dough for the mattress.

Flatten a smaller sausage of dough for the pillow. Pinch out the corners.

Roll a ball for the head and place in dent in pillow. Add a sausage for the body.

Fold over one end.

Make sheet larger than bed.

Make pattern on sheet with end of straw or pen top.

Cut out a rectangle from thinly-rolled dough.

Roll two sausages for arms. Add some balls for hands.

Make rug as on page 6.

Place the sheet over the body. Add the arms and some hair and mark in the eyes and mouth. See left for how to make teddy and other details.

Other ideas to try

Teddy bear
Roll a small ball for his head, two tiny balls for his ears and one for his nose. Join two small sausages for arms. Mark in his eyes with a pencil.

Hot-water bottle
Flatten a small ball of dough into a disc. Add a smaller ball for the neck of the bottle. Press a pencil in the end for an opening.

Book
Cut a thick rectangle from rolled dough. Mark pages on three sides with a knife.

15

Special occasions

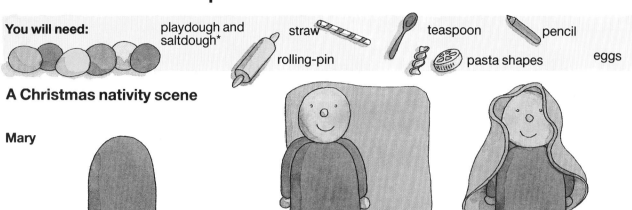

You will need: playdough and saltdough* rolling-pin straw teaspoon pencil pasta shapes eggs

A Christmas nativity scene

Mary

Roll a short, fat sausage for her body, so she will look as if she is kneeling.

Add arms, hands and a head. Mark in her mouth and eyes. Flatten a ball of dough for her cloak.

Drape the cloak over her head and body, so it lies in folds behind her.

Joseph and shepherd

Cut down a straw for a stick.

Give them taller bodies. For the shepherd roll a long, thin headband.

For gifts cut cubes from thickly-rolled dough and decorate with pasta shapes.

To make sheep see page 5.

Crib

Roll a fat sausage. Press a bent finger firmly into the centre. Roll four thin sausages for crosses at each end.

Three kings

You can add a feather.

Give them brightly coloured cloaks. Make headbands by joining balls of dough, or twisting sausages.

Make the baby Jesus as shown on page 8. Put him in the crib.

16

round-ended knife   plate   baubles and holly   candle   ribbon   cookie cutters   wool   fork

Christmas log candle-holder

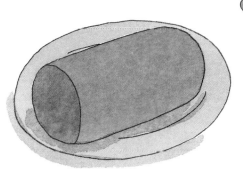

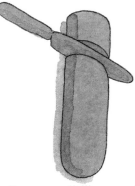

Roll a fat, long sausage for the log. Cut each end with a knife and put on a plate.

Roll a small "branch". Cut one end off diagonally, before joining it to the log.

Scratch in a bark pattern with a fork and mark the rings at each end with a teaspoon.

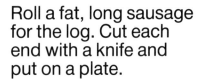

Don't use ribbon, it might catch fire.

Push a candle firmly into the log and then decorate it with baubles and holly.

Saltdough tree shapes

Roll dough out thinly. Cut out shapes with cookie cutters or a round-ended knife. Poke a hole in each one. Bake and paint*.

*To find out how to make, bake and decorate saltdough, see page 30.

Easter ideas

Egg faces

Roll a ball of dough and stand it on a plate. Press a hard-boiled egg into it, pointed end down. Add hair, faces and hats.

Hen on a nest

Make a hen by pressing together the parts shown above.

Make a disc of dough. Roll lots of thin sausages. Twist them together, then press them round the disc to form the sides.

Roll some coloured eggs to put in the nest.

17

Halloween party decorations

You will need:
pencil
playdough — rolling-pin
candle
spoon
plate
round-ended knife

Skull centre-piece

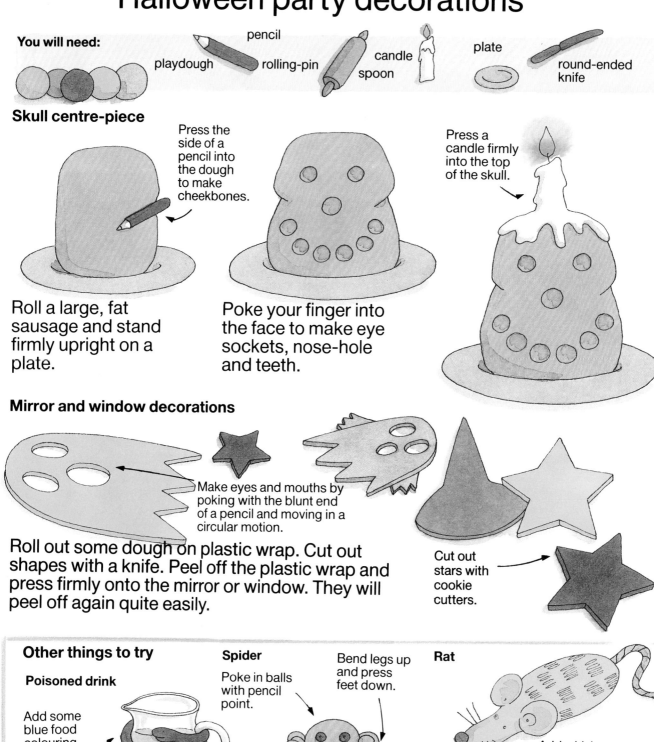

Press the side of a pencil into the dough to make cheekbones.

Roll a large, fat sausage and stand firmly upright on a plate.

Poke your finger into the face to make eye sockets, nose-hole and teeth.

Press a candle firmly into the top of the skull.

Mirror and window decorations

Make eyes and mouths by poking with the blunt end of a pencil and moving in a circular motion.

Roll out some dough on plastic wrap. Cut out shapes with a knife. Peel off the plastic wrap and press firmly onto the mirror or window. They will peel off again quite easily.

Cut out stars with cookie cutters.

Other things to try

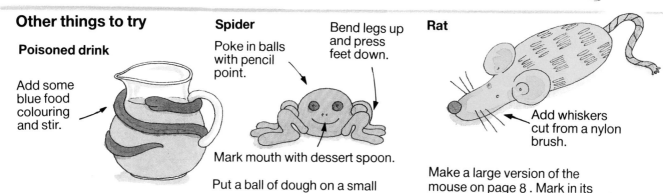

Poisoned drink

Add some blue food colouring and stir.

Wind a long playdough snake around a glass jug of lemonade.

Spider

Poke in balls with pencil point.

Bend legs up and press feet down.

Mark mouth with dessert spoon.

Put a ball of dough on a small plate. Add some sausages for legs.

Rat

Add whiskers cut from a nylon brush.

Make a large version of the mouse on page 8 . Mark in its fur with a fork and add string for a tail.

18

 serving bowl

 pasta shapes

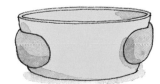 glass jug

 string

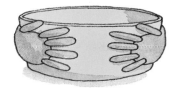 plastic wrap

 torches

Ghostly hands

Roll two golf ball sized pieces of playdough.

Flatten them onto the outside of a large serving bowl.

Add four sausage-shaped fingers and a shorter thumb.

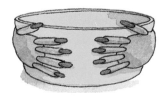

Press some smaller sausages onto the ends of the fingers for nails.

Use the bowl to serve chips or crackers.

Add a pasta shell "ring" and mark in the finger joints by pressing with a knife.

Spooky flashlight

Press a ball of dough over the centre of the face of a flashlight. Make a face by pressing in the flat end of a pencil and moving it in a circular motion until a hole appears; mark the eyes, nose and mouth. Shine the light in the dark for a spooky effect. Try flashing it on and off quickly.

Dinner on a plate

You will need:

playdough

rolling-pin

children's scissors

round-ended knife

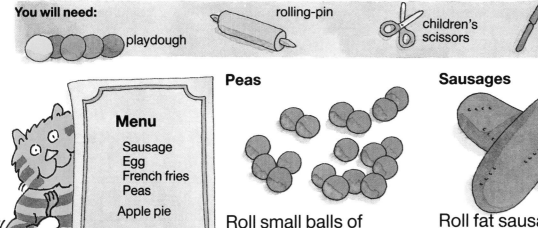

Menu

Sausage
Egg
French fries
Peas

Apple pie

Peas

Roll small balls of green dough and press them lightly together.

Sausages

Roll fat sausages of brown dough. Prick them with a fork.

Eggs

Flatten a ball of white dough. Press a smaller ball of yellow on the top for the yolk.

French fries

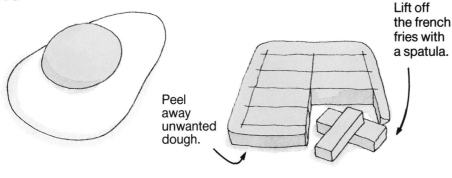

Peel away unwanted dough.

Lift off the french fries with a spatula.

Roll some dough out thickly and cut in straight lines across and downwards.

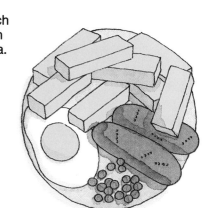

Arrange the food on a plate.

Other things to try

Hot dog
Make a bread roll with two sausage shapes of dough. Sandwich a sausage in the middle.

Olive

Sweetcorn

Pizza
Press out some dough to almost cover a small plate. Decorate with shapes cut from rolled dough and small rolled balls.

Fish sticks
Cut from thick, orange dough, as for french fries above. To make a crumby surface, scratch with a fork.

Peppers

fork

 plastic wrap

 plates

 spatula

Pastry pie with roses

Press out or pat a large ball of dough onto a plate, turned upside-down, for the pie-crust.

Pinch round the edge to make a wavy pattern, or press the knife-blade gently all round the edge to decorate.

Snip some steam-holes in a pattern with some scissors.

Pastry roses

Roll out some dough and cut into long strips, one for each rose.

Roll up the strips. Pinch the pastry together near the base of the roll.

Cut off bottom.

Pull the outside pastry gently outwards to look like wavy petals.

Cut out some leaves. Mark them with a knife and arrange on top of the pie with the roses.

Jellies and other ideas

Press playdough into wetted molds and gently pull it out. Use small jelly-molds or bun trays. Roll a red cherry to decorate.

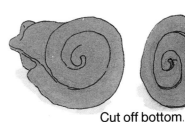

Ice cream
Press balls of dough into a dish. Roll small red balls for cherries. Cut out a wafer with a knife.

Happy birthday cake
Make a big birthday cake, decorate it and add some candles. After the candles and singing cut the cake into slices.

Bread and cakes

You will need: saltdough*   rolling-pin   pencil   paint   round-ended knife   felt-tip pen

Swiss roll

Peel away unwanted dough.

Roll out dough thinly. Cut a rectangular shape.

Lift one short edge gently with a knife. Roll up the dough.

Glaze and bake. Draw in the jam with felt-tip pen.

Fruit cake

Flatten a ball of dough, then poke it with a pencil point. Bake and paint.

Jam tarts

Roll small balls of dough. Press the flat end of a pencil into the centre of each. Glaze, then bake them.

Paint the centres red to look like jam.

Chocolate eclairs

Roll out two long sausages. Press one lightly on top of the other. Bake and paint them.

Hints

Place the items on the baking tray before molding and glazing.

Remember to remove any plastic from bottle lids before cooking.

Serve on plates made from jam-jar lids, lined with doilies or paper towel cut to fit.

  *To find out how to make, bake and decorate saltdough, see page 30.

 lightly-oiled baking tray

 metal bottle-top

 doilies or paper towels

 plates

 plastic wrap

Cherry buns

Roll small balls of dough.

 Add a tiny ball for a cherry.

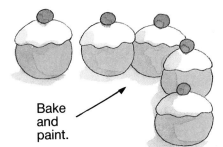

Flatten small balls between your fingers for icing.

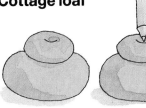

Bake and paint.

French sticks

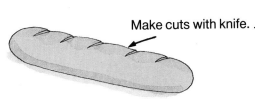

Make cuts with knife.

Roll a long sausage. Glaze and bake.

Granary loaf

Roll a ball of dough. Glaze, bake and paint.

Cottage loaf

Roll a ball of dough. Add a smaller ball and poke in with a pencil.

Rolls and crackers

Mark with a pencil.

Roll small balls of dough for rolls. For crackers flatten them between your fingers.

Pies

Don't fill it right to the top.

Roll a ball of dough and press into a bottle lid.

Decorate it with a small ball of dough. Mark it with a straw. Bake and paint.

Scones

Dip pen top in flour before cutting.

Squeeze to release dough.

Roll out some dough, not too thinly. Cut out some scone shapes with a pen top. Bake.

Baker's shop

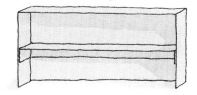

Cut a 1 in strip from the long side of the box lid, to make a shelf.

Cover the sides of the shelf with glue and press it firmly into the lid.

Glue the lid onto the back of the upturned box to a depth of 1in.

Ideas for your shop

Bread baskets Use individual sections of an egg carton or cut-down yoghurt pots.

Price tickets Stick small pieces of card onto toothpicks. Press into a ball of dough.

Wrappers Thread small squares of tissue paper or paper towel with wool. Make a hole with a pencil point in the side of the counter. Poke a toothpick in to make a hook. Hang the wrappers up.

Try making a butcher's shop with hams, chops and sausages, or a fish stall with lots of different fish.

Cut out a piece of card, write the shop name on it, and glue it to the top of the lid at the back.

Allow the glue to dry, then paint the shop. Line the shelf with paper towel or doilies, glued in position. Arrange your bread and cakes.

Picnic food

You will need: saltdough* round-ended knife drinking straw paints felt-tip pens egg glaze (see page 29) pastry cutters or aerosol can lids paper towels round-ended scissors

Sausage rolls

Roll small sausages then press a straw into each end to make the filling.

You could use a felt-tip pen to colour the filling brown.

Make cuts across the top with a knife. Glaze them, then bake them.

Cheeses

For holey cheese prick with a pencil point.

Flatten a ball into a disc. Cut wedges. Bake, cool, then paint.

Sandwiches

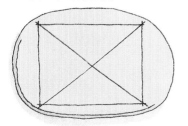

Roll out dough about ½in thick. Cut a square with a knife, then cut into quarters.

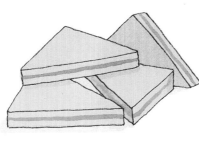

Separate the four pieces and bake. Draw a felt-tip line round each piece for the filling.

Ideas for your picnic

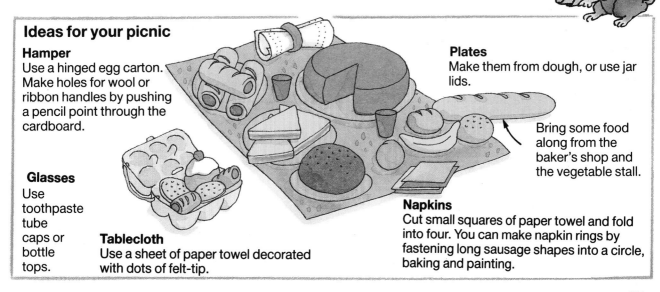

Hamper
Use a hinged egg carton. Make holes for wool or ribbon handles by pushing a pencil point through the cardboard.

Glasses
Use toothpaste tube caps or bottle tops.

Tablecloth
Use a sheet of paper towel decorated with dots of felt-tip.

Plates
Make them from dough, or use jar lids.

Bring some food along from the baker's shop and the vegetable stall.

Napkins
Cut small squares of paper towel and fold into four. You can make napkin rings by fastening long sausage shapes into a circle, baking and painting.

To find out about making and baking saltdough, see page 30.

Fruit and vegetable stall

You will need: 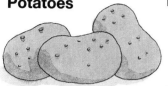 round-ended knife  lightly-oiled baking tray oven gloves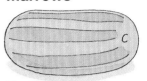

saltdough* pencil cellophane tape paint felt-tip pens

cooling tray egg boxes card and glue

Potatoes

Roll small balls. Squash into knobbly shapes. Mark eyes with pencil point.

Peppers

Roll short, fat sausages. Make criss cross marks with a knife across the top.

Cucumbers

Roll long sausages, thinner at one end than the other. Make long marks lengthways with a knife.

Marrows

Roll fat sausages. Draw in stripes with felt-tip pens.

Cauliflower

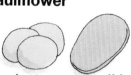

Push three small balls of white dough together. Flatten small green balls of dough to make leaves. Overlap the leaves round the centre. Mark the centre with a pencil point.

Carrots

Roll sausage shapes thinner at one end. Add some green leaves and make marks around the carrots with a knife.

Apples

Roll small balls and poke a pencil point into the tops.

Bananas

Roll sausage shapes and curve them. Draw on felt-tip markings.

Oranges

Roll small balls. Mark peel with pencil point.

Spring onions

Roll very skinny sausages and press them together into bundles. Colour the ends green.

Glue on a sign for the stall.

my stall

Put all your fruit and vegetables into an egg box.

Hint

These items are small and will bake hard in around 20 minutes at gas mark 4, 180°C (350°F).

Use cut-down sections of egg box for additional baskets.

To find out about making, baking and colouring saltdough, see page 30.

26

Using playdough as a mold

You will need:  plaster-of-paris, playdough, rolling-pin, paint, brush, plastic jug, jar lids, water, round-ended knife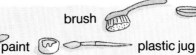

Badge

Roll out a disc of playdough at least 1½in thick. Press the jar lid firmly into the dough to make a round well.

Collect some small objects, such as the ones above, from around the house. You could also use small plastic toys.

Press the objects into the playdough inside the well. Don't press them too deep. Lift them out carefully.

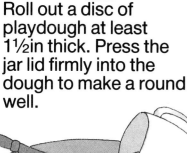

Leave to set for 10 to 15 minutes.

Mix up the plaster and pour it into the well. Gently slap the surface with a knife to get rid of air bubbles.

When dry, carefully pull off the playdough. Scrub the plaster clean with a scrub brush, under a tap.

Allow to dry thoroughly, then paint. Fix a safety-pin on the back with adhesive bandage (see page 7).

Other things to try
Name plaque
Roll out some dough quite thickly and press a date-box lid upside down into it to make a frame.

Write your name on greaseproof paper and turn it over to use as a pattern.

Press plastic letters into the dough, following the pattern. Pour in plaster. Allow it to set. Scrub and paint.

Hand molds
Press your foot or outspread hand into a thick piece of rolled-out dough. Lift it out carefully to leave a clear outline. Pour in plaster and leave it to set.

Allow to dry thoroughly, then paint.

Hint
Don't dispose of wet plaster down the sink. Put it in a plastic bag, allow it to set, then put it in the trash can.

Dough shapes you can eat

You will need:

1 packet/ 283gms/ 10oz of plain white bread-mix

pastry brush

pencil

1 egg beaten with 1 tbsp of water

child's scissors

round-ended knife

oiled baking-tray

spatula

teaspoon

cooling rack

oven gloves

flour

plastic wrap

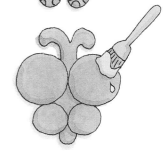

When you have made the shapes you want, leave them to rise in a warm place for between 30 and 55 mins. Glaze them then bake as specified on packet.

Butterfly

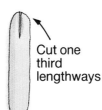

Cut one third lengthways

Roll a long sausage. Snip one end with some scissors

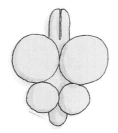

Make wings by flattening balls. Press them onto the body.

Curl the snipped dough round to make antennae.

Tortoise

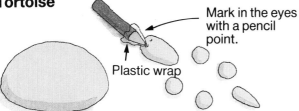

Mark in the eyes with a pencil point.

Plastic wrap

Mark the shell with a knife.

Pat a piece of dough into a dome shape.

Roll out shapes for a head, legs and tail.

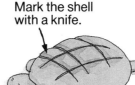

Lift up the edges and tuck the feet, head and tail underneath.

Hints
Where pieces of dough need joining, dip a finger in water and wet both surfaces.
Work directly onto the baking tray to avoid spoiling shapes when you move them.
Always handle the dough on a lightly-floured surface.

Octopus

Press on eyes with pencil point.

Mark mouth with teaspoon.

Roll a fat sausage and press it out into an oblong.

Make tentacles by snipping with scissors.

Pull down tentacles and curl around.

Other ideas
Try the snake on page 9, or the hedgehog on page 10.

Letter buns
Using sausage shapes of dough make the letters of your name.

28

Playdough and saltdough

You can buy playdough in toyshops or department stores or you can make it yourself. You simply mix the ingredients and heat them on a stove, or in a microwave oven.

If you want to make things that will go hard so you can keep them and play with them, you need to use saltdough.

To make saltdough you combine the ingredients without cooking them. When you have made what you want you can harden it by baking it in the oven.

The things you will need for each project in the book are listed across the top of each page. Sometimes playdough is specified, sometimes saltdough with baking and painting instructions. However, if you want to you can do all the projects with playdough or with saltdough.

How to make playdough

Ingredients:

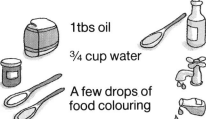

1 cup flour

½ cup salt

2 tsps cream of tartar

1tbs oil

¾ cup water

A few drops of food colouring

- Put the flour, salt, cream of tartar and oil into a large saucepan.
- Add the food colouring to the water.
- Add the liquid gradually to the ingredients in the saucepan and mix it in thoroughly to get rid of as many lumps as possible.
- Put the pan over a medium-low heat and cook, stirring constantly. This is quite hard work. The mixture will be very liquid at first, then begin to thicken suddenly.
- Continue to stir until the dough becomes very stiff.
- Remove the pan from the heat and scrape out the dough with a wooden spoon onto a smooth surface.
- Put the pan to soak immediately.

Warning: playdough looks very tempting at this stage, but the inside will still be very hot, even when the outside has cooled. Before using, slice it in half with a knife and test it carefully with your finger.

- Knead it thoroughly until it becomes smooth and pliable and holds its shape well.

Using a microwave

This method involves much less physical effort and produces excellent results. The instructions given are for a 650 watt oven. Adjust accordingly.

- Mix the ingredients as for pan-cooked playdough (see below left) but use a large bowl suitable for microwave use.
- Put the bowl, uncovered in the microwave.
- Cook at full power for one minute.
- Using oven gloves remove it from the oven and stir well.
- Replace the bowl and continue cooking until the mixture starts to leave the side of the bowl and becomes very stiff – approximately 2-2½ minutes. (Stir at least once during this time.)
- Using oven gloves, remove from the oven onto a heatproof surface.
- Scrape out the dough with a wooden spoon onto a smooth surface.
- Knead as before.

Storing playdough

Playdough needs to be kept in an airtight container to stop it drying out.

Bought playdough should keep indefinitely when stored in its pot with the lid firmly on.

Store homemade playdough in a polythene food bag, inside an airtight box or jar.

If left exposed to the air a salty crust will form on it. You can rescue it by kneading it thoroughly with a little oil.

Colour mixing

You can create most of the colours you might want by mixing blue, scarlet and yellow. If you have pink and green as well it extends your range considerably.

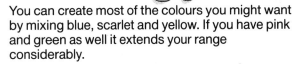

Blue + scarlet = brown

Blue + pink = purple/mauve

Blue + yellow = green

Yellow + scarlet or pink = orange

Scarlet + green = warm shades of brown

Green + yellow = acid green

Green + blue = dark leaf green

Experiment with different combinations. Mix colours on saucers first, before adding them to the water.

Build up a library of colours. Make smaller quantities of those you think you will use least.

The colour will not come out onto your hands during use, but it is advisable to keep it off carpets.

Saltdough

Saltdough recipe
Ingredients:

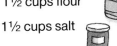

1½ cups flour

1½ cups salt

1 tbs oil

Approximately
½ cup water

- Mix all the ingredients in a large bowl using a knife. The dough should feel pliable – add more liquid if necessary.
- Turn out onto a floured surface and knead thoroughly until very smooth and elastic.

Saltdough improves with keeping. Its texture becomes finer and less grainy. It is best made the day before you need it.

Warning
Salt can sting. Protect small cuts and scrapes on the hand with adhesive bandage.

Storing saltdough
The uncooked dough keeps indefinitely in a plastic bag in the fridge. If it goes a little soft, knead some flour into it before use.

Colouring saltdough
You can colour saltdough while you are making it by adding food colouring to the mixing water. The colour will go a little lighter when the dough is baked.

Where small quantities of coloured dough are needed, as for the vegetables on page 26, mix the colours you want on separate saucers, then knead in small portions of white uncooked dough until evenly coloured.

Painting
Instead of using food colouring you can paint saltdough after it has been baked. Use powder, poster or watercolour paints.

You could just add the finishing touches with paint or felt-tip pens.

Painting will soften the dough temporarily. Allow it to dry out again in the air or still warm oven. Place painted items on a cake cooling rack to dry quickly without spoiling.

Glazing
This gives dough a lovely golden brown colour. Try it for the miniature breads on page 23.

Simply beat a whole egg and paint onto the uncooked saltdough with a pastry brush or paintbrush.

Baking saltdough

Cook small items for between 10 and 20 mintues, depending on their size, on a lightly-oiled baking tray or roasting pan at gas mark 4, 350F, 180C in the centre of the oven.

Larger items are best cooked overnight at gas mark ½, 250F, 130C. This avoids the dangers of cracking or the dough beginning to brown on the outside while the centre is still uncooked. Precoloured dough may brown very slightly on cooking. The dough is also liable to balloon out of shape if cooked at too high a temperature.

Don't worry if the inside is still a little spongy even after cooking overnight; the salt in the dough acts as a preservative and the centre will air-dry and harden after a while. The larger and thicker the item the longer the drying-out time will be.

You can safely bake small items with larger ones overnight at a low temperature.

Do not use thin trays or cake pans if cooking overnight; they will brown and spoil and scorch coloured dough.

There may be some cracking if your oven is too hot. This is usually underneath the piece and does not spoil the look of the finished article. Experience will tell you how the dough behaves in your own oven.

Saltdough expands slightly on cooking. Keep this in mind while shaping. Make good-sized holes for threading, so they don't close up during baking.

Microwave ovens are not suitable for baking saltdough. The dough tends to balloon out of shape and the salt burns easily.

Always warn of the dangers of a hot oven or baking tray and make a noticeable display of wearing oven gloves.

Tools

Surfaces to work on

Work on smooth surfaces such as formica or polyurethaned wood, or turn trays upside down so that the rim does not get in the way. You can also work on large flat books wrapped in plastic wrap.

Playdough rolled out onto a piece of plastic wrap lifts and peels off beautifully, leaving a lovely smooth surface on the underside.

When working with saltdough lightly dust the surface with flour.

Tools you may need

 A rolling-pin. You could use a piece of dowelling, or a broom handle instead, or use one from a child's baking set.

Knives. For safety always use round-ended ones. Plastic knives are safe and light to handle.

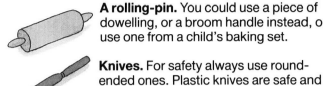 **Scissors.** For safety use round-ended ones and child-sized ones for easy use. Use for snipping raised patterns (e.g. the hedgehog's quills on page 10), or cutting dough cleanly to mark in mouths and so on.

Forks. Use for scratching or pressing patterns into the dough, or for scratching two surfaces to be joined. Plastic forks are light and easy to handle, but be careful the prongs are still sharp.

 Spoons. These are very useful for marking curved mouth shapes. Use the side of a dessert-spoon for a large mouth and the tip of a teaspoon for a small one.

 Sieve. A large-meshed metal one is best. These can be used to push dough through so it forms fine strings. Push clumps gently together to make bushes (page 5), or hair for figures or animals. It may help to wet the sieve, shaking off excess water, to enable the dough to be pushed through more easily.

Use the sieve also for washing small objects, like buttons or beads, which are smeary after being pushed into dough. Put them in the sieve, then swish them around in warm soapy water. Rinse them under the tap, then turn them out onto a kitchen roll to dry.

 Pencil. This is very useful for pressing in eyes with the pointed end, making patterns with either end, or pressed sideways into the dough. Alternatively use a child's knitting needle.

 Cutters. Use cookie cutters, upturned plastic tumblers, or plastic tops from aerosol cans (flour lightly before use, squeeze gently to release dough). Plastic pen tops make tiny cutters (e.g. for miniature scones on page 23).

 Spatula. This is useful for lifting and transferring pieces without damage, or removing hot saltdough items from baking tray to cooling rack, or pressing patterns into dough.

 Other tools. Straws, toothpicks, keys, pasta, beads, buttons, shells, pebbles. Anything which will make a clear imprint in dough can be used to build up a pattern.

 Molds. Small bun trays or jelly molds can be used. Push dough firmly into the wetted mold. Ease away from the sides and pull out gently to make "cakes" and "jellies". Try using the molded plastic containers from chocolate or toy-packaging.

 Use playdough itself as a mold. Impressions can be made in the dough and a cast taken with plaster (see page 27).

Techniques

Starting off
Once they have learned how to make some simple basic shapes children will soon be able to decide how to go about putting their own ideas into practice. The projects in this book are mostly created from varying sizes of ball shapes or sausage shapes.

Rolling balls

Show children how to pinch off a piece of dough and press it into a rough ball shape.
- Place it on the flat palm of an open hand.
- Lay the other hand on top and roll gently between the palms with a circular motion.
- Turn the ball a few times in between rolling until you have a good shape.
- Or place the roughly-shaped ball onto a smooth surface and roll with a circular movement under your open palm.
- To roll several balls of the same size pinch off a piece of dough, divide it into two, then divide each piece in two, and so on until you have the number you want. This way you can make ears, feet and so on that match in size.
- Tiny balls for noses, buttons and so on can be rolled in the palm of your hand with a finger tip. The ball will stick to the end of your finger; lift gently and press in position.

Discs

- These can be made by patting a ball evenly with the palm of your hand, or flattening a ball directly onto the model with a finger. You can also roll out the dough and cut a shape, using a suitably sized cutter.

Rolling sausage-shapes
- Break off a piece of dough, then roll it into a ball shape. Either roll the ball gently between the palms of your hands, or place on a smooth surface and roll lightly back and forward.
- Long sausage-shapes can be rolled using two hands at once, with closed fingers. Move from the centre outwards as you roll, to lengthen the dough.
- Or roll with the palm of the hand on first one section, then another, to keep thicknesses even.
- Rolling to a pointed end (for tails etc.) Roll out a sausage shape, then continue to roll at one end only with most pressure on the outside of your palm, until a point is formed. A really fine point can be made by continuing to roll with a finger tip.

Rolling out dough
- Form the dough into a rough ball with your cupped hands, then place on a smooth surface. Pat it out into a thick disc with your open palm, then roll your rolling-pin forwards and back using both hands until it becomes the thickness you want. Rolling out on plastic wrap helps you turn the dough easily to be rolled in another direction.
- To roll long thin shapes make a sausage shape and roll out as above.

Using cutters
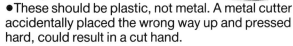
- These should be plastic, not metal. A metal cutter accidentally placed the wrong way up and pressed hard, could result in a cut hand.
- Press the cutter gently into the dough with the flat of your hand, then more firmly once it has bitten. Wriggle it slightly from side to side to make sure it has cut right through.
- Lift off the unwanted dough from round the cut shape. This leaves it free to be lifted elsewhere on a spatula, or decorated.

Free-hand cutting
This is best done with a round-ended knife, preferably plastic.
- Roll the dough out evenly and draw the shape you want onto it with the knife, before cutting.
- You can use a paper pattern as a guide. Lay it on the dough and cut round it.
- Use a ruler to help you cut straight lines.
- Don't try to turn a corner in the dough with the knife. Make each cut longer than you need, criss-crossing at the corners each time to leave the shape you require (see page 2, caterpillar on a leaf).

Joining pieces of dough
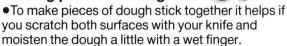
- To make pieces of dough stick together it helps if you scratch both surfaces with your knife and moisten the dough a little with a wet finger.
- You can use a piece cut from a drinking straw to help you join pieces.
- Another way of joining two pieces of dough is to shape one into a point and make a hole in the other piece for a point to fit into.

Decorating dough

This can be done in a variety of ways: poking with fingers, pinching, pressing with various parts of the hand, making imprints with a variety of objects (see tools) or decorating with buttons, beads or pasta. Experiment with anything which makes a sharp outline or interesting shape.